Spot the Differences

Search & Find Fun

Illustrated by Genie Espinosa

Dover Publications, Inc.
Mineola, New York

Bibliographical Note

This Dover edition, first published in 2019, is a slightly
altered republication of the work illustrated by Genie
Espinosa and written by Paul Virr, which was originally
published by Arcturus Publishing Limited, London,
in 2018.

International Standard Book Number

ISBN-13: 978-0-486-83231-9
ISBN-10: 0-486-83231-7

Manufactured in the United States by LSC Communications
83231701   2019
www.doverpublications.com

PIZZA PUZZLE

Find ten differences at this pizza restaurant.
Circle the changes in the picture at the bottom.

ROBOT FACTORY

Whirr! Clang! Beep! Everyone is busy at the robot factory.

Get to work and circle ten differences at
the robot factory in the scene below.

DINO DIFFERENCES

Take a safari and go dinosaur watching.

Find and circle ten differences in the scene below.

FUN AND GAMES

It's so much fun at the fair!

Find and circle ten differences in the picture below.

PLANE SPOTTING

Find and circle ten differences in the
bottom scene before takeoff!

FUN IN THE SUN

Make a splash at the beach! Find and circle
ten differences in the bottom image.

FEEDING TIME

What a lot of hungry animals!

Find and circle ten differences in the petting zoo picture below.

PIRATE SHIP

Ahoy there, shipmate! Today we are making believe we are pirates.

Circle ten differences below, or Captain Bluebeard
will make you walk the plank!

ALL ABOARD

Quick! The train is about to leave the station.

Can you spot and circle ten differences
in the scene below so you don't miss the train?

CRAZY GOLF

Can you spot and circle ten differences in the bottom picture?
Give it your best shot.

PONY PUZZLE

Saddle up! Find and circle ten changes
in the bottom picture.

KINDERGARTEN

Everyone's having fun at kindergarten today!

Join in and see if you can spot and circle
ten differences in the picture below.

AUTO REPAIRS

Pass the wrench and help to fix these cars!

Find and circle ten changes at the workshop below.

CANDY STORE

Everything here looks yummy!

Can you spot and circle ten differences
in the sweet scene below?

SPACE SPOTTER

This scene is out of this world! Find and circle
ten changes in the bottom picture.

FIRE STATION

Emergency! Race to the rescue and circle
ten differences in the bottom picture.

AMAZING AQUARIUM

Dive in and see all the amazing sea life at the aquarium.

Find ten differences between the two underwater scenes.
Circle the changes below.

ROAD RUNNERS

Go as fast as you can in this fun road race!

Find ten differences and circle them in the picture below.

LET'S PLAY!

Have fun finding ten differences in these playtime scenes.
Circle the changes in the bottom picture.

PLENTY OF PETS

Find and circle ten differences at the pet store in the bottom scene.

AT THE MALL

Get ready to shop and be with friends at the mall.

Find and circle ten differences in the scene below.

TRICK OR TREAT?

It's Halloween and everyone is wearing a fun costume.

Find and circle ten differences in the spooky scene below.

SNOWY DAY

Have a really cool time with this snow scene.
Find and circle ten changes in the bottom picture.

POOL PUZZLE

Splish, splash! Find and circle ten differences
in the pool scene at the bottom.

JUNGLE FUN!

These animals are having a blast in the jungle.

Go exploring and see if you can spot and circle
ten changes in the picture below.

TOY STORE

Wow! Look at all the different toys.

Find and circle ten changes in the toy store picture below.

ARCTIC ANTICS

Brrrr! Chill out by circling ten differences in the bottom scene.

MARKET DAY

It's time to shop today! Find and circle ten differences in the picture at the bottom.

MAGIC SHOW

Abracadabra! The magicians are putting on a wonderful show.

Find and circle ten changes in the magic show scene below.

ICE AGE ESCAPADES

Travel back in time to the Ice Age.

Can you find and circle ten differences in the picture below?

FOREST FRIENDS

It's a lovely day for a walk in the forest.

Can you spot and circle ten differences in the forest scene below?

SCHOOL BUS

Time for school. Find and circle ten changes
in the bus scene on the bottom

GARDEN FUN

Find and circle ten differences in the garden scene on the bottom.

ONCE UPON A TIME

It's story time and all the characters are looking for a happy ending.

Find and circle ten differences in the fairy-tale scene below.

ON SafaRI

There are lots of animals to spot on a safari.

Find ten changes in the picture of the
safari scene below. Circle them.

SUPER SPLAS ⬛ !

Are you ready to make a big splash?

Find and circle ten changes in the water park picture below.

PRETTY PETS

Spot ten differences between these pampered pet pictures and circle them on the bottom.

WaSHDaY FUN

Get those clothes clean! Spot and circle ten differences
in the picture on the bottom.

AMUSEMENT PARK

Hold on tight, this is going to be fun!

Can you find ten differences on this page? Circle them below.

UNDER THE SEA

There's so much to see under the sea.

Find and circle ten differences in the undersea scene below.

CRAZY KITCHEN

Slice, dice, and spot ten differences in the kitchen!
Circle the changes in the picture on the bottom.

FLYING HIGH

Search the sky for ten differences between these scenes.
Circle the changes in the picture on the bottom.

COSTUME PARTY

Dressing up is so much fun!

Find and circle ten differences in the party scene below.

TAKE A BREAK

It's time to take a break from schoolwork.

Can you find and circle ten changes in the picture below?

CORAL REEF

Dive into the sea and explore the coral reef.

What ten things have changed as the sea creatures
swim along in the scene below? Circle them.

TIME FOR TEA

Spot ten differences between these tea party scenes.
Circle the changes in the bottom picture.

74

CHIC SALON

It's busy at the salon today. Find and circle
ten differences in the bottom picture.

MAKING MOVIES

Many people are needed to make a movie.
You could be the star of the show!

Spot and circle ten differences in the movie scene below.

HAPPY NEW YEAR!

It's party time—we are celebrating Chinese New Year!

Find and circle ten differences in the scene below.

ZANY ZOO

Follow the road around to see all the animals at the zoo.

Find and circle ten differences in the zoo picture below.

DESERT TOUR

Can you spot ten differences in the desert?
Circle the changes in the scene on the bottom.

GLADIATOR SCHOOL

Travel back in time to Ancient Rome. Can you spot and circle ten differences in the bottom scene?

CHRISTMAS TIME

It's time to decorate the Christmas tree!

Spot ten differences and circle them in the festive scene below.

SUPERHERO PARTY!

You're invited to a superhero birthday party!

Use your awesome powers to spot and circle
ten differences in the picture below.

BUSY BUILDERS

Spot ten differences between these construction sites.
Circle the changes in the picture on the bottom.

ANSWERS!

3 PIZZA PUZZLE

10 PLANE SPOTTING

4–5 ROBOT FACTORY

11 FUN IN THE SUN

6–7 DINO DIFFERENCES

12–13 FEEDING TIME

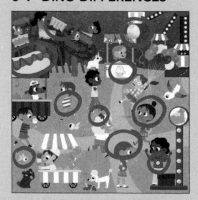

8–9 FUN AND GAMES

14–15 PIRATE SHIP

16-17 ALL ABOARD

18 CRAZY GOLF

19 PONY PUZZLE

20–21 KINDERGARTEN

22–23 AUTO REPAIRS

24–25 CANDY STORE

26 SPACE SPOTTER

27 FIRE STATION

28–29 AMAZING AQUARIUM

30–31 ROAD RUNNERS

32 LET'S PLAY!

33 PLENTY OF PETS

34–35 AT THE MALL

36–37 TRICK OR TREAT?

38 SNOWY DAY

39 POOL PUZZLE

40–41 JUNGLE FUN

46–47 MAGIC SHOW

42–43 TOY STORE

48–49 ICE AGE ESCAPADES

44 ARCTIC ANTICS

45 MARKET DAY

50–51 FOREST FRIENDS

52 SCHOOL BUS

53 GARDEN FUN

60 PRETTY PETS

54–55 ONCE UPON A TIME

61 WASHDAY FUN

56–57 ON SAFARI

62–63 AMUSEMENT PARK

58–59 SUPER SPLASH!

64–65 UNDER THE SEA

66 CRAZY KITCHEN

67 FLYING HIGH

68–69 COSTUME PARTY

70–71 TAKE A BREAK

72–73 CORAL REEF

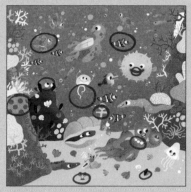

74 TIME FOR TEA

75 CHIC SALON

76–77 MAKING MOVIES

78–79 HAPPY NEW YEAR!

84–85 CHRISTMAS TIME

80–81 ZANY ZOO

86–87 SUPERHERO PARTY!

82 DESERT TOUR

88 BUSY BUILDERS

83 GLADIATOR SCHOOL